RAINBOW
magic®

The Party Fairies

For Saoirse Medway

Special thanks to
Sue Mongredien

ORCHARD BOOKS

First published in Great Britain in 2005 by Orchard Books
This edition published in 2017 by The Watts Publishing Group

3

© 2017 Rainbow Magic Limited.
© 2017 HIT Entertainment Limited.
Illustrations © Georgie Ripper 2005

A CIP catalogue record for this book is available from the British Library.

ISBN 978 1 40834 865 9

Printed in Great Britain

The paper and board used in this book are made from wood from responsible sources

Orchard Books
An imprint of Hachette Children's Group
Part of The Watts Publishing Group Limited
Carmelite House, 50 Victoria Embankment, London EC4Y 0DZ

An Hachette UK Company
www.hachette.co.uk
www.hachettechildrens.co.uk

Cherry
the Cake
Fairy

by Daisy Meadows

illustrated by Georgie Ripper

Join the Rainbow Magic Reading Challenge!

Read the story and collect your fairy points to climb the
Reading Rainbow at the back of the book.

This book is worth 5 points.

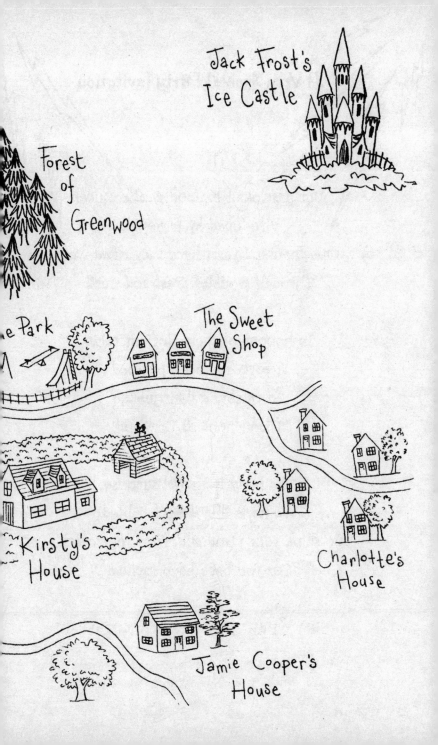

A Very Special Party Invitation

Our gracious King and gentle Queen
Are loved by fairies all.
One thousand years have they ruled well,
Through troubles great and small.

In honour of their glorious reign
A party has been planned,
To celebrate their jubilee
Throughout all Fairyland.

The party is a royal surprise,
We hope they'll be delighted.
So shine your wand and press your dress...
For you have been invited!

RSVP: HRH THE FAIRY GODMOTHER

Contents

A Birthday Surprise

"I just know this is going to be
a wonderful birthday!" Kirsty Tate
exclaimed happily, her eyes shining.

Mrs Tate laughed across the breakfast
table. "You've only been awake
for half an hour, Kirsty," she said.

"I know," Kirsty replied. "But
look at all these cards I've been sent!

And there's my party this afternoon. And best of all, Rachel's here for a whole week!" She grinned at her best

friend, Rachel Walker, who was sitting next to her. The two girls were spending a week of the Easter holidays together. They had met on holiday the year before and, since then, they had had all kinds of magical adventures together. First, they had helped all seven of the Rainbow Fairies return to Fairyland. Then, they'd helped the Weather Fairies stop wicked Jack Frost from causing weather chaos!

The girls finished their breakfast and went to get dressed. Rachel was halfway up the stairs behind Kirsty, when she noticed another envelope coming through the letterbox. She ran to get it. It was a very grand-looking, sparkly gold envelope, and it felt heavy in her hand. She glanced at the front curiously – and then gasped in surprise.

Miss Kirsty Tate and Miss Rachel Walker, the beautiful loopy handwriting read. Rachel blinked. A card for Kirsty *and* for her? It wasn't her birthday for another three months!

She raced up the stairs, two at a time, puzzling it over. She didn't recognise the handwriting, so it couldn't be from her mum or dad. But who else knew that she was staying with Kirsty?

"Look," cried Rachel, bursting into Kirsty's bedroom. "Another card – and it's for both of us!"

Kirsty took the envelope and gently turned it over, running her finger around the red wax seal on the back. "You open it," she said, passing the letter back to Rachel. "I've had all my other cards this morning."

Rachel's fingers trembled with excitement as she carefully broke the wax seal. As soon as the envelope was open, glittering clouds of fairy dust billowed into the air, followed by a rainbow of colour that soared across the room.

Both girls stared, open-mouthed.
Riding on top of the rainbow, just as
if he was surfing on a wave, was
Bertram, the Fairyland frog footman!
Rachel and Kirsty had met him before
in their fairy adventures. But they
hadn't expected to see him again in
Kirsty's bedroom.

Bertram hopped off the rainbow onto
Kirsty's chest of drawers and bowed
deeply. He wore a red waistcoat and
carried a gold bugle.

Kirsty grabbed Rachel's hand excitedly
and squeezed it. She couldn't help
wondering if this would be the start of
another magical quest!

Bertram tooted on the bugle, then
pulled a tiny scroll from one of his
pockets. He unrolled it, and cleared his
throat. "Ahem. It is with great
pleasure," he began,
"that I bring you
good news. The
Fairy Godmother
hereby invites
Kirsty Tate and
Rachel Walker to a
surprise party – for
the Fairy King and
Queen's 1000th jubilee!"

"Wow!" gasped Rachel.

"Yes, please!" Kirsty cried.

From another of his pockets, Bertram
pulled out a tiny bag of fairy dust and
began sprinkling it over Kirsty's mirror.

As the girls watched, the mirror's reflection vanished and a whole new scene appeared before their eyes.

"It's Fairyland!" Rachel breathed, leaning closer for a better look.

"Correct," said Bertram. "The Fairy Party Workshop, to be precise. All the Party Fairies have been working very hard to make sure the King and Queen's party is absolutely perfect."

Kirsty and Rachel gazed in delight at the small figures they could see bustling around in the workshop.

"There's Cherry the Cake Fairy, making
a special party cake," Bertram told
them, pointing a webbed green
finger. The cake did
indeed look wonderful.
It was shaped like a fairy
palace and it sparkled
with magic. "That's
Grace the Glitter Fairy,
making lots of magical
decorations. And can
you see the fairy
wrapping up gifts so
prettily? She's Jasmine
the Present Fairy."

The two girls watched in
delight as Jasmine tied a pink satin
bow around one of the presents.
"Who else is there?" Kirsty asked eagerly.

Bertram pointed. "There's Polly the Party Fun Fairy. She's in charge of party games. And Melodie the Music Fairy sorts out the best party tunes. She's teaching the fairy orchestra how to play the harmonies for 'Happy Jubilee'." The girls fell silent and listened to the sweet sounds of fairy music tinkling through the mirror. "It's gorgeous," Rachel sighed. Bertram went on. "Honey the Sweet Fairy is making sure there are enough treats to go round, and Phoebe the Fashion Fairy – she's the one with the extra-sparkly wings, look – is in charge of everybody's party outfits."

Kirsty gazed in wonder at the beautiful dress Phoebe was working on. It was covered with hundreds of sequins and jewels that glittered in the light. "It's lovely," breathed Kirsty, her eyes wide with excitement. "And we're really invited to the party?"

"Oh, yes," Bertram replied. "The Fairy Godmother says that you and Rachel will be special guests."

"Special guests!" Rachel echoed, looking thrilled at the thought.

"So, when is the party? And how will we get there?" Kirsty asked.

Bertram murmured something at the mirror and the Fairyland scene dissolved into hundreds of twinkling stars, before finally disappearing.

"The party's at the end of the week. And the Fairy Godmother will send a magic rainbow to collect you," he said. He handed the magic invitation to Rachel. "To get to Fairyland, all you have to do is step into the end of the rainbow," he explained, "like this."

Kirsty and Rachel watched as
Bertram placed one froggy foot,
then another, into the colourful
rainbow that hovered in the air.
And then – *whoosh* – with a shower
of golden fairy dust, he was gone.

"Hurrah!" exclaimed Kirsty. "I knew this was going to be a brilliant birthday."

Fun and Games

Rachel and Kirsty got dressed, chatting excitedly.

"'Special guests', the Fairy Godmother called us," Rachel said proudly, tying up her hair in a band. "Imagine! You and me, special guests of the Fairy King and Queen!"

"It's amazing," Kirsty grinned, brushing her hair. "I can't wait to go to Fairyland again."

Just then, there was a shout from downstairs. "Come on, girls!" Mrs Tate called. "There's lots to do before the party starts."

Rachel and Kirsty looked at each other in amazement. How did Mrs Tate know about the Fairyland party? Then Kirsty chuckled. "She means my party," she said. "Do you know, I'd almost forgotten all about it!"

The girls laughed and hurried downstairs. In the kitchen, Mr Tate was icing Kirsty's birthday cake. "There," he said, putting nine candles on top. "It's all finished."

"That looks delicious, Dad," Kirsty said, hugging 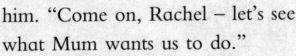 him. "Come on, Rachel – let's see what Mum wants us to do."

Mrs Tate soon had the two girls making up party bags for all of Kirsty's guests. Then they blew up lots of pink and lilac balloons to hang from the ceiling. And finally there was just time for the girls to put on their party dresses before the guests arrived.

"Musical Statues first," Mrs Tate
announced to all the girls gathered in the
lounge. "When
the music stops
– so do you!"
The music
started and
everybody
danced. Then
Mr Tate switched
it off – and
everybody froze
on the spot. Rachel
was standing on one
leg, trying to keep as
still as possible, when she suddenly saw
swirls of red and purple glitter floating
through the doorway. She stared in
surprise, wondering what it could be.

Then she flicked her eyes to the side, wondering if Kirsty had spotted the glitter, too. Kirsty's startled expression told Rachel that she had, but none of the other children seemed to have noticed anything unusual.

The sparkling dust floated up to Rachel, drifting right under her nose. "Atishoo! Atishoo! Atishoo!" she sneezed.

Now the dust was under Kirsty's nose, too. It was so ticklish, she just couldn't help rubbing her nose.

"Rachel and Kirsty – you two are out!" Mrs Tate said. "Here comes the music again."

As quickly as they had appeared, the swirls of red and purple glitter vanished. Rachel frowned at Kirsty. "What was that?" she hissed as they went to sit down.

Kirsty grabbed her arm and steered her towards the door. "I think it might have had something to do with her," she whispered, pointing through the doorway.

Rachel followed Kirsty's finger, and a broad smile spread over her face. For there, hovering in mid-air and waving at the girls, was a tiny sparkling fairy!

Stop Thief!

"You're one of the Party Fairies!"
Rachel exclaimed as they rushed over to
speak to the fairy. "We saw you in
Bertram's picture."

The fairy smiled. She had lovely, deep
violet eyes and long, dark, curly hair,
tied in bunches with red ribbons. She
wore a red skirt, a pink wrap-around

top, red party shoes and stripy socks.
From her wrist, swung a sparkly red
party bag. "I certainly am," she replied,
with a little curtsey. "I'm Cherry the
Cake Fairy."

An anxious
frown creased
her forehead.
"I'm sorry if my
fairy dust spoiled
your game," she went on,
"but I really need your help!"

"Of course!" Kirsty said at once.

"Whatever's happened?" Rachel asked.

Cherry smiled gratefully. "Well, you
see, as the Cake Fairy, whenever a party
is in danger of being ruined by a spoiled
cake, I get called away from Fairyland
to fix it. And today, I've been very busy.

One of Jack Frost's goblins has been spoiling birthday cakes all over the country. He steals the cake candles, and stomps in the icing." She bit her lip. "And he's on his way to Kirsty's party right now!"

Rachel's mouth fell open. "What a cheek!" she exclaimed.

Kirsty glanced over to the kitchen door. "Why is the goblin spoiling all the cakes?" she asked. "And what can we do to stop him?"

Cherry's eyes flashed. "Nobody knows what the goblin is up to," she told the girls. "But one thing's for sure — if Jack Frost's behind it, it's bound to be something bad." She shrugged. "All we can do is try to catch the goblin before he causes any more trouble."

"What are we waiting for?" Rachel cried. "Let's stand guard over Kirsty's cake at once!"

The girls raced to the kitchen, with Cherry fluttering along behind. As soon as they opened the kitchen door, though, they knew that they were too late. All the candles had been pulled out of Kirsty's cake, and there were goblin footprints in the icing.

"Oh, no!" cried Kirsty in dismay. "He's ruined it!"

"He's taken all the candles, too," Rachel added crossly.

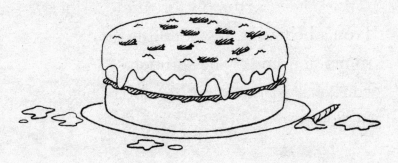

"And I'll take this, as well!" they heard somebody cackle. And before anyone could stop him, a grinning green goblin jumped out from behind one of the table legs, snatched Cherry's party bag out of her hands and ran off, laughing nastily.

A Tricky
Problem

"Hey!" Cherry cried. "Give that back!"

Kirsty and Rachel stared in horror as the goblin ran away. He was his normal size, Rachel noted with relief. She remembered that the Fairy King and Queen had taken Jack Frost's magic away for one year, after his mean mischief had nearly ruined Christmas.

Clearly, his punishment meant that he
hadn't been able to cast a spell to make
the goblins super-sized like he'd done
once before. An enormous rucksack
bumped up and down on the goblin's
back. It was stuffed full of party candles.

"We've got to get my party bag
back!" Cherry cried, flying after the
thief. "Quick!"

The goblin was just about to dodge out of the kitchen door, when Kirsty's kitten, Pearl, came bounding into the room. As soon as Pearl saw the goblin, she fluffed up her black and white fur in alarm and hissed.

The goblin's eyes bulged in panic and he skidded to a halt. Then he climbed up to one of the kitchen cupboards and locked himself in!

Cherry flitted about anxiously. "That party bag has got all my magical fairy dust inside," she fretted. "I need that to help make parties perfect – and to finish off the King and Queen's jubilee cake."

Rachel banged on the cupboard door. "Give that party bag back to Cherry this minute!" she ordered the goblin.

"No chance," the goblin shouted back sulkily. "It's mine now – and as soon as I get out of here, I'll be giving it to Jack Frost."

"What does he want it for?" Kirsty asked curiously.

The goblin gave a gloating chuckle. "For his party of course," he replied. "The King and Queen said he's got to stay in his ice castle, but they didn't say he couldn't have a party – and a very grand one it's going to be, too!

Now that I've got this party bag of magic dust, his cake is going to be the most splendid cake you ever saw." There was another cackle of glee from the cupboard. "Just you wait – once we've got all the Party Fairies' party bags, Jack Frost will use the magic dust, instead of his own magic, to make his party extra-special."

Cherry had turned quite pale. She beckoned the girls back over to the table, where they huddled together to hear her whisper.

"It's bad enough that he's got my party bag when I haven't finished the King and Queen's cake," she said. "But if the goblins are planning to steal all the magical party bags, then none of the Party Fairies will be able to finish their work in time for the jubilee."

She shook her head miserably. "The surprise party will be ruined!"

A Sticky Solution

The girls thought hard to try and find a way of recovering Cherry's party bag. But they couldn't think of anything.

"The Fairy Godmother is much more powerful than a goblin," Cherry sighed. "She'd soon sort all this out if only I could get the goblin back to Fairyland.

But I can't magic him there while he's in that cupboard – or while he's running away. I need him to keep fairly still, so that I can wave my wand over him."

Kirsty found her gaze drifting towards her ruined birthday cake. "Poor Dad spent ages on that icing," she said sadly.

Then she grinned suddenly as a thought struck her. "That's it!" she muttered. "That's how we'll catch him out!" "How?" Rachel asked blankly.

"We need to make more icing for this cake," Kirsty said loudly. She took out a box of icing sugar and started mixing some icing in a bowl.

Then she added quietly, "Cherry, could you use some fairy magic to make this icing extra-sticky?"

"No problem," Cherry replied. She waved her wand over the bowl and a stream of sparkling purple 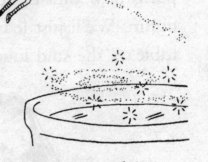 and red fairy dust swirled around it. The white icing glittered for a split-second and strange red and purple sparks crackled above it. Then it turned a glossy white again.

Kirsty gave one last stir and smiled. "Super-sticky!" she whispered.

Rachel was still frowning. "I don't—" she began.

But Kirsty put a finger to her lips. "It's a trap!" she whispered into Rachel's ear. Quickly, she covered the cake with the new icing. "We'd better get back to the party now that the cake's all right again. We'll just leave it here on the table..." she said loudly.

Rachel and Cherry followed Kirsty out of the room. Holding their breath, they waited outside the kitchen, peeping through the crack in the door to see if Kirsty's trap would work. Sure enough, after a moment, the cupboard door creaked open and the goblin climbed down and skipped gleefully across the floor. Grinning nastily, he climbed up onto the kitchen table, and then made a massive leap straight onto the top of the newly-iced cake.

"There he goes," Kirsty whispered to Rachel. "And any second now, he'll realise..."

"I'm stuck!" the goblin howled suddenly. "They've tricked me!"

"Perfect timing," chuckled Cherry. The goblin was stuck fast, unable to move his feet in the super-sticky icing. Rachel laughed out loud at his furious face. "Brilliant idea, Kirsty," she cheered.

Cherry flew over to the goblin,
her eyes on her precious
party bag, but he
bared his teeth at
her. "Any closer,
fairy, and
I'll bite you!"
he warned.

"In that case,
I'll have to
take you back
to Fairyland,"
Cherry said calmly.
"And won't the Fairy Godmother be
interested to hear what you and Jack
Frost have been plotting?"

The goblin scowled, but said no more.

"Serves you right for ruining my
cake – twice!" Kirsty couldn't help adding.

"Don't worry about your cake, Kirsty," Cherry said. "Once I've got my party bag back, I'll magic you the most beautiful birthday cake you've ever seen. Now, I don't suppose you two would like to come to Fairyland with me, would you?"

"Yes, please!" Kirsty cried at once, but Rachel was glancing up at the kitchen clock.

"What about your party, Kirsty?" she pointed out. "Musical Statues must be about to end soon."

Cherry twirled her wand around. "Don't worry," she said, "I'll work some magic so that it will seem as if you've only been gone from the party for a moment. Will that help?"

"Oh, yes!" cried both girls together.

"I was hoping you'd say that," Cherry smiled. "Off we go!"

A Magical Mystery Cake!

With a blur of bright colours – and the delicious smell of freshly baked cakes – Kirsty and Rachel found themselves whizzing through the air towards Fairyland.

"Hello," they heard a sweet voice calling as they landed with a bump. "Which one of you is Kirsty and

which one is Rachel? I've heard so
much about you, my dears."

Kirsty and Rachel blinked and looked
around. They were back in Fairyland,
and were now fairy-sized themselves.
And there, standing in front of them, was
somebody who could only be the Fairy
Godmother. She had long copper hair
swept up into a ponytail, the kindest
green eyes that Rachel and Kirsty had
ever seen, and wings that shimmered

every time they moved. Her long
golden dress was covered in tiny
glimmering jewels that twinkled all
the colours of the rainbow.

"I'm Kirsty," Kirsty said, jumping
up at once.

"And I'm Rachel," Rachel added,
scrambling to her feet.

"Delighted to meet you at last,"
the Fairy Godmother replied,
dropping a beautiful curtsey.

Then her eyes narrowed at the sight of the goblin, standing next to Cherry. "I see that you've taken something that doesn't belong to you," she said sternly, pointing a finger at Cherry's party bag.

Whizz! The party bag glowed with red and purple light and shot out of the goblin's hands at once. It zoomed straight over to Cherry, who clutched it with relief.

"Thank you!" she cried.

"You're welcome, my dear," the Fairy Godmother said. Then she fixed

her gaze on the goblin. "As for you, I've got just the thing to teach you a lesson." She pointed a finger at him. "You'll need that," she said, "and that." Kirsty and Rachel couldn't help laughing as an enormous chef's hat suddenly appeared on the goblin's head, and a crisp white apron wrapped itself around his body.

"You can help in the Party Workshop for the rest of the week, icing all the cakes," the Fairy Godmother went on firmly.

"Let's hope that keeps you out of mischief."

The goblin looked very sulky as Cherry bustled him away. "You won't catch the other goblins so easily," he snarled. "We'll get the rest of those party bags, just you wait and see!"

Once he'd gone, the Fairy Godmother turned back to Kirsty and Rachel. "I'm afraid he might be right," she told them. "Jack Frost's goblins can be very cunning, as you know. They'll try every trick they can think of to steal the other magical party bags."

"What can we do to help?" Kirsty asked at once.

The Fairy Godmother smiled and sighed. "All you can do is look out for trouble at parties," she said. "The goblins are likely to try and spoil human parties because they know that the Party Fairies will rush to help.

That will give them the chance they need to steal the fairies' party bags."

"We'll keep a look-out," Rachel promised.

At that moment, Cherry returned. "We'd better send you back to your party," she told the girls. "And don't worry – I'm sure there won't be any more goblins to spoil your fun today." She carefully opened her party bag and reached inside. Then, just as the

Fairy Godmother pointed her wand at the girls and called, "Home!" Cherry threw a handful of red and purple fairy dust over them.

The world seemed to spin, there was a sweet, sugary smell in the air and then the girls found themselves back in Kirsty's kitchen.

"Jessica's the winner!" they heard Mrs Tate saying. "Come and get your prize for being the best statue, Jessica."

"It sounds like the game's only just finished," Kirsty said happily. "Just like Cherry promised. Let's go and join the party again, Rachel."

But Rachel was staring at the kitchen table in wonder. "Look, Kirsty!" she gulped. "Look at your cake!"

Kirsty gasped in surprise. The red and purple fairy dust that Cherry had thrown over them was floating down onto the cake that Mr Tate had made. As the girls watched, they realised that the fairy dust was actually red and purple hundreds and thousands, and as they landed on the cake something amazing happened. A delicious fragrance of vanilla and sugar floated around the room, and the

original cake melted into thin air, while
a new cake formed in its place. Kirsty
and Rachel stared in wonder as
three tiers appeared, one by
one, beautifully covered
with white, pink and
lilac icing. Each tier
was decorated with
tiny sugar fairies,
twining sugar roses
and shiny silver bells.
Kirsty broke the silence
with a sudden laugh. "It's
the Party Fairies!" she cried,
pointing at the sugar figures.
"There's Cherry with a wooden spoon,
see? And the Glitter Fairy, didn't Bertram
say her name was Grace? And a fairy with
a present – that must be Jasmine. And— "

Suddenly, they heard Mrs Tate calling for them. "Kirsty! Rachel! Where are you?"

"Time to go," Rachel said. "Shall we take the cake in with us, just to be on the safe side?"

"Good idea," said Kirsty. Then she grinned. "I can't wait to see everybody's faces!"

Very carefully, the girls lifted the magnificent cake. As they carried it

into the living room together, the little silver bells tinkled merrily.

"Wow!" cried Kirsty's friend Jessica. "I've never seen anything like it."

Another girl, Molly, was licking her lips. "It's almost too beautiful to eat," she said. "Although it smells so gorgeous, I'll give it a try!"

Mrs Tate looked dazzled. "It's a work of art!" she said to her husband in amazement.

Mr Tate was staring at the cake, too, with a bewildered expression on his face. "Well... Um... It's not so difficult when you know how," he said sheepishly.

"I can't wait to see what you're going to do for my birthday next month!" Mrs Tate added. Mr Tate looked rather alarmed at that, so Kirsty interrupted quickly.

"Shall we cut the cake, Mum?"

"Good idea," Mrs Tate replied. She lit the candles, and everybody sang 'Happy Birthday'. Then Kirsty carefully sliced into the lowest tier of the cake.

As she did so, hundreds of magical butterflies fluttered out into the room, their colourful wings sparkling in the sunshine.

"Ooooh!" everybody exclaimed, as the butterflies vanished into thin air. "Just like magic!"

Kirsty and Rachel smiled at each other. They both knew that it *was* magic – fairy magic, the most wonderful magic in all the world!

As they tucked into slices of the delicious birthday cake, they both thought of their new fairy mission with excitement.

"I can't wait to meet the other Party Fairies," Rachel whispered to Kirsty. "But I'm not looking forward to seeing any more goblins."

"I know," Kirsty agreed. "I just hope we can stop them from spoiling the King and Queen's party."

Rachel patted her friend's arm comfortingly. "At least Cherry said there'd be no more trouble at your party," she pointed out. "So we can enjoy the rest of your birthday without worrying."

Kirsty nodded. "Yes," she said. Then she grinned. "An invitation to the King and Queen's jubilee party, meeting Cherry and a visit to Fairyland – I just knew this was going to be a wonderful birthday," she sighed happily, "and I was right."

**Now Rachel and Kirsty
must help...**

Melodie the Music Fairy

Read on for a sneak peek...

"Kirsty, you're a brilliant dancer!" Rachel Walker smiled, clapping her hands as her friend took a bow. Kirsty had just finished practising the ballet steps she would be performing later that evening.

"It will look even better tonight, with the other dancers and the proper costumes," Kirsty replied with a grin. "And wait till you hear the lovely music."

Rachel was staying with her best friend, Kirsty Tate, for the week. That evening, the girls were going to the village hall for a special occasion – the first anniversary of

Kirsty's ballet school.

"It's going to be a great party," Kirsty went on. "My ballet teacher is decorating the hall and organising some games, and all the parents are bringing food."

"It sounds fun," Rachel agreed. "But if it's a party, then we'll have to be on the lookout for goblins!"

Kirsty nodded. She and Rachel shared a magical secret: they were friends with the fairies! But, right now, there were problems in Fairyland and Kirsty and Rachel had promised to help.

The fairies were planning a surprise celebration for the 1000th jubilee of the Fairy King and Queen. It was meant to be taking place in five days' time, and the Party Fairies were in charge of making it as special as possible using their party bags of magic fairy dust.

But nasty Jack Frost had other plans. Banished to his ice castle by the Fairy King and Queen, he had decided to throw a party of his own on the very same day. Jack Frost knew that whenever a party in the human world went wrong, the Party Fairies would fly to the rescue...

Read Melodie the Music Fairy
to find out what adventures are in store for Kirsty and Rachel!

Meet the Party Fairies

Cherry the Cake Fairy

Melodie the Music Fairy

Grace the Glitter Fairy

Honey the Sweet Fairy

Polly the Party Fun Fairy

Phoebe the Fashion Fairy

Jasmine the Present Fairy

When Jack Frost steals the Party Fairies' magical bags, Kirsty and Rachel must come to the rescue before parties everywhere fizzle into flops!

www.rainbowmagicbooks.co.uk

Calling all parents, carers and teachers!
The Rainbow Magic fairies are here to help
your child enter the magical world of reading.
Whatever reading stage they are at, there's
a Rainbow Magic book for everyone!
Here is Lydia the Reading Fairy's guide to
supporting your child's journey at all levels.

1 Starting Out

Our Rainbow Magic Beginner Readers are perfect for first-time readers who are just beginning to develop reading skills and confidence. Approved by teachers, they contain a full range of educational levelling, as well as lively full-colour illustrations.

2 Developing Readers

Rainbow Magic Early Readers contain longer stories and wider vocabulary for building stamina and growing confidence. These are adaptations of our most popular Rainbow Magic stories, specially developed for younger readers in conjunction with an Early Years reading consultant, with full-colour illustrations.

3 Going Solo

The Rainbow Magic chapter books – a mixture of series and one-off specials – contain accessible writing to encourage your child to venture into reading independently. These highly collectible and much-loved magical stories inspire a love of reading to last a lifetime.

www.rainbowmagicbooks.co.uk

"Rainbow Magic got my daughter reading chapter books. Great sparkly covers, cute fairies and traditional stories full of magic that she found impossible to put down" - Mother of Edie (6 years)

"Florence LOVES the Rainbow Magic books. She really enjoys reading now" - Mother of Florence (6 years)

The Rainbow Magic
Reading Challenge

Well done, fairy friend – you have completed the book!
This book was worth 5 points.

See how far you have climbed on the **Reading Rainbow**
on the Rainbow Magic website below.

The more books you read, the more points you will get,
and the closer you will be to becoming a Fairy Princess!

How to get your Reading Rainbow
1. Cut out the coin below
2. Go to the Rainbow Magic website
3. Download and print out your poster
4. Add your coin and climb up the Reading Rainbow!

There's all this and lots more at
www.rainbowmagicbooks.co.uk

You'll find activities, competitions, stories, a special
newsletter and complete profiles of all the
Rainbow Magic fairies. Find a fairy with your name!